An Archway
Overlooking
A Garden
At A Home
In Tangier

FACES
AND
PLACES

MOROCCO

BY PATRICK MERRICK

THE CHILD'S WORLD®, INC.

GRAPHIC DESIGN AND PRODUCTION
Robert E. Bonaker / Graphic Design & Consulting Co.

PHOTO RESEARCH
James R. Rothaus / James R. Rothaus & Associates

COVER PHOTO
Portrait of a Moroccan girl
©Arthur Thévenart/CORBIS

Library of Congress Cataloging-in-Publication Data
Merrick, Patrick.
Morocco / by Patrick Merrick.
    p. cm.
Includes index.
Summary: Introduces the history, geography, people,
and customs of the North African nation of Morocco.
ISBN 1-56766-737-6 (lib. reinforced : alk. paper)

1. Morocco Juvenile literature. [1. Morocco.] I. Title.

DT305.M495 2000
964 — dc21
                                            99-40504
                                              CIP
                                              AC

Table of Contents

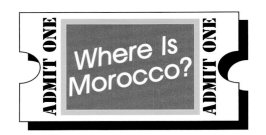

Where Is Morocco?

Of all the planets in the solar system, Earth is special. That is because Earth is the only planet with water. Most of the water can be found in huge oceans on Earth's surface. But Earth also has large land areas. The seven big areas of land on Earth are called **continents**. One of the largest of these continents is Africa.

Western Hemisphere

Eastern Hemisphere

Both Morocco (white) And U.S.A. (green) Are In The West

There are many fascinating countries in Africa. One of these countries is Morocco.

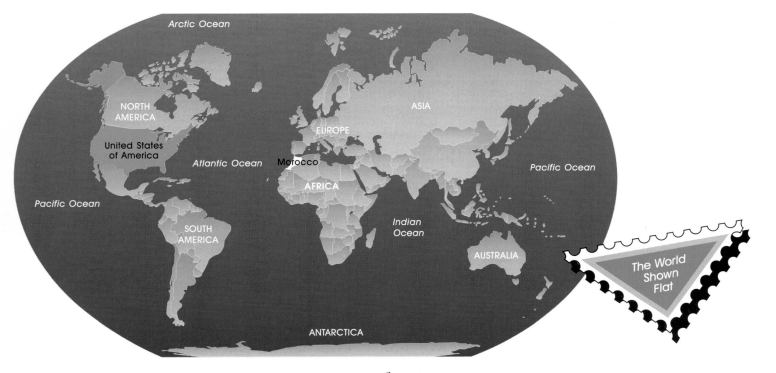

Arctic Ocean

NORTH AMERICA

United States of America

Atlantic Ocean

Morocco

ASIA

EUROPE

Pacific Ocean

AFRICA

Pacific Ocean

SOUTH AMERICA

Indian Ocean

AUSTRALIA

The World Shown Flat

ANTARCTICA

PORTUGAL

SPAIN

Mediterranean Sea

Strait of Gibraltar

Atlantic
Ocean

MOROCCO

CANARY
ISLANDS

ALGERIA

WESTERN
SAHARA

MAURITANIA

MALI

Close-Up
of
Morocco

A Crowded Beach In Rabat

Tangier
★ Rabat
ATLAS MOUNTAINS
• Asni
SAHARA DESERT

©Chinch Gryniewicz; Ecoscene/CORBIS

A Man Riding Through The Atlas Mountains Near Asni

©K. M. Westermann/CORBIS

Morocco is a wonderful land. Within its borders, you can live in many different types of places. For those who like mountains, Morocco has the *Atlas Mountains* which have some of the prettiest views in Africa. These mountains have beautiful woodlands and peaceful river valleys. Around the mountains are huge flat areas called **plains**.

Sand Dunes Reflected In A Sahara Desert Lake

People who like the ocean love the long, sandy beaches along the Atlantic Ocean and the Mediterranean Sea. For those who like sand, there are miles and miles of sand in the famous *Sahara desert*.

A Moroccan Desert Cactus In The Sahara Desert

Because there are so many different types of land, there are also many different types of plants and animals. Morocco's warm, sunny weather helps all kinds of trees to grow.

Pine, cedar, and eucalyptus trees grow in some regions. So do olive trees and cork trees. The plains have many different grasses. Farther south, large cacti grow in the desert.

A Barbary Ape In Northern Morocco

©Robert Gill; Papilio/CORBIS

Each different area has strange and wonderful animals. In the mountains, there are **mouflon**, or mountain sheep. On the plains, gazelles run free. In the forests, you can see monkeys. In the desert, there are camels.

©Roger Tidman/CORBIS

©K. M. Westermann/CORBIS

Tamri

SAHARA
DESERT

Tree
Goats Near
Tamri

Roman
Ruins
At
Volubilis

∴ VOLUBILIS RUINS
• Casablanca

Casablanca Was Bombed In 1942 During World War II

©Hulton-Deutsch Collection/CORBIS

People have been living in Morocco for thousands of years. Some of the earliest people lived in groups and were called **Berbers**. Others were called *Arabs*. Because Morocco is in a position to keep boats from getting into and out of the Mediterranean Sea, many powerful countries have tried to **conquer** it.

Moors Load A Cannon During The Spanish-Moroccan War In 1923

©Hulton-Deutsch Collection/CORBIS

In the past, the Romans, Portuguese, Spanish, and French have all tried to take over Morocco. Every time people from another country came to Morocco, they brought their beliefs and customs. Finally, in 1956, Moroccans gained their independence. Because of its long history, Morocco now has a rich culture with many interesting traditions.

Morocco Today

Today, Morocco has a king who rules over the country. He is working hard to keep Morocco a good place to live or visit. Every year thousands of people travel to Morocco to enjoy its interesting sights.

A Royal Guard In Rabat

©Robert Holmes/CORBIS

However, like many places in the world, there are places in Morocco that different people claim as their own land. One of these places is an area to the south of Morocco called *Western Sahara*. The people of Western Sahara believe that they are their own country. Many people in Morocco don't want Western Sahara to become independent. They want Western Sahara to stay part of Morocco.

The Government Center In Rabat

©Robert Holmes/CORBIS

Rabat ★ • Fès

The Gates
Of The
King's
Palace
In Fès

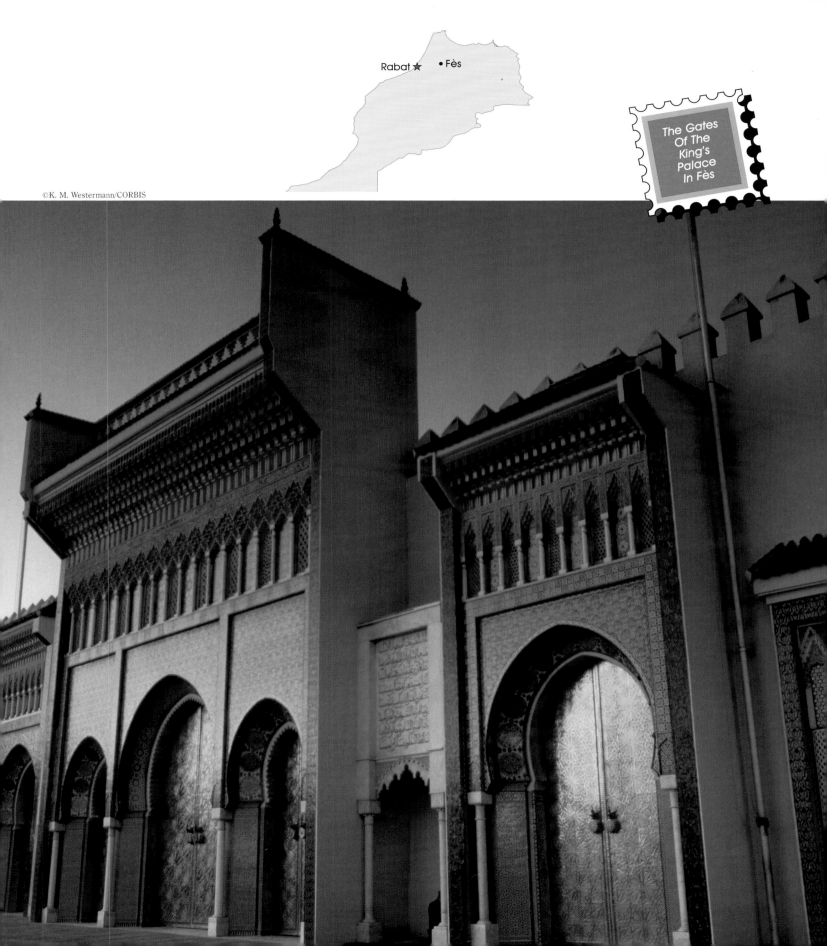

Men
Talking
At A
Market In
Tangier

•Tangier

• Fès

The People

Most Moroccans of today are still related to the Berber or Arabic people who were in the country thousands of years ago. To most Moroccans, their *Islamic* religion is very important.

The population of Morocco is getting bigger. This means that there are a lot of young people living in Morocco. Most people there are under the age of 20. In fact, if you were to walk around in Morocco, one out of every three people you met would be a child.

©Dave G. Houser/CORBIS

A Berber Woman And Her Children In Fès

A Merchant At A Market In Tangier

©Owen Franken/CORBIS

Men Walking In A Market In Casablanca

©Roger Wood/CORBIS

Most Moroccans live in the country. They live in mountain villages or on small farms. One important part of country life is the **souk**. The souk is an open-air market where Moroccans can trade for things they need.

A Village In Dades Gorge

©Christine Osborne/CORBIS

Morocco also has many large cities. Casablanca is the largest city in Morocco and one of the biggest in all of Africa. Life in Casablanca is like life in most large cities. There is always something new to see or do!

• Casablanca

⊙ DADES GORGE

Modern
Buildings
In
Casablanca

A
Business
School In
Settat

• Settat

©Tom Thistlethwaite; Ediface/CORBIS

Moroccan children go to school just as you do. In school, they learn how to read, write, and do math and science. They also have fun playing games and singing songs. In Morocco, most children go to elementary school, but very few go on to high school.

A Stop Sign In Arabic

An Arabic Sign In Morocco Points The Way To Tombouctou In The Country Of Mali

In Moroccan cities, most people speak *Arabic*, Morocco's official language. Some people also speak French or English. In smaller villages, some people still speak the native Berber languages their relatives spoke hundreds of years ago.

©Roger Antrobus/CORBIS

A Man Repairing Fishing Nets In Safi

©Robert Holmes/CORBIS

There are many different jobs in Morocco. Most Moroccan people are either fishermen or farmers. In the country, farmers grow rice, cotton, fruits, and many other foods. Morocco also has many mines. Morocco has more of an important rock called **phosphate** than any other place in the world.

©K. M. Westermann/CORBIS

In the city, people work in restaurants, shops, and factories. Moroccan factory workers produce everything from clothes and furniture to plastics and machines. Everyone is very busy in Morocco!

Women Decorating Pottery in Fès

©Paul Almasy/CORBIS

• Fès

• Safi

Young Berber Shepherds In The Moroccan Countryside

A Bowl
Of Couscous
And Vegetables
In Tangier

•Tangier

•Fès

©Michelle Garrett/CORBIS

Food

Moroccan people love good food. When they cook, they like to use lamb, beans, and flavorful spices. The most famous dish in Morocco is **couscous**. This is a dish made with beans, spices, and vegetables or meat. Couscous is the national dish of Morocco and is usually eaten last at a meal.

Almost everyone in Morocco drinks tea. It is served all the time and is usually flavored with mint or orange. Tea is often served with honey and nut pastries such as cake, cookies, and other goodies.

©Craig Aurness/CORBIS

Men Having Tea At Fantasia Festival In Fès

©Michelle Garrett/CORBIS

Fresh Fish And Vegetables In Tangier

Pastimes and Holidays

ADMIT ONE   ADMIT ONE

Moroccans like to spend time outside. They enjoy swimming, golfing, hunting, or simply taking a nighttime stroll in the city. The most popular sport in Morocco is soccer, which is also the national sport. Soccer matches draw very large crowds of excited fans.

Moroccans also love music. Traditional songs are sung in small shops, while more modern music can be found in the larger towns. In the country, many people still sing the Berber music of their ancestors. Along with singing, Moroccans love to dance.

Moroccans celebrate many holidays. The most important is the *Festival of the Throne* on March 3. This is the anniversary of the day the Moroccan king took power. This holiday has fireworks, parades, dances, and food. All over Morocco, smaller holidays also are celebrated. On these days, people enjoy music, dancing, and games.

From games and parades to quiet nights and beautiful scenery, Morocco has something for everyone. From the beaches to the mountains, Morocco will give you a visit you will never forget!

A Storyteller Playing A Flute In Fès

Meknes • • Fès

• Marrakech

+ TOUBKAL MOUNTAIN

A Battle Reenactment During The Festival Of The Throne Celebration Near Meknes

Area
Almost 173,000 square miles (447,000 square kilometers)—about twice as big as Minnesota.

Population
About 28 million people.

Capitol City
Rabat.

Other Important Cities
Casablanca, Fès, and Tangier.

Money
The dirham.

National Languages
Arabic. French, English, and several native languages are also spoken.

National Song
"Al Nachid Al Watani," or "The National Anthem of Morocco."

National Flag
Solid red with a green star in the middle. The star is known as "Solomon's seal." Green is the traditional color of the religion of Islam.

Head of Government
The king of Morocco.

Morocco Trivia

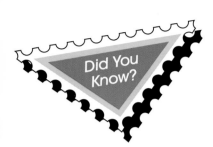

Did You Know?

Morocco is really called "The Kingdom of Morocco." People just say "Morocco" for short.

To show hospitality, Moroccans often give their guests a tray of dates and milk.

Toubkal Mountain in Morocco is the tallest point in northern Africa.

Many Moroccans do not drink anything during a meal. Only after the table has been cleared do they serve tea.

How Do You Say?

HOW TO SAY IT IN ARABIC

Hello	AH–hlan
Good-bye	MAH ahs–sah–LEH-mah
Please	MIN FAHD–lak (to a man)
	MIN FAHD–lik (to a woman)
Thank You	SHUK–rahn
One	WATT–hid
Two	ITH–nayn
Three	THAH–lih–thah
Morocco	el–MAH–greb

Berbers (BUR–burz)
The Berbers are people who have been living in Morocco for a long time.

conquer (KAHNG–ker)
When someone conquers something, they take it by force. Many countries have tried to conquer Morocco.

continents (KON–tih–nents)
Most of Earth's land lies within huge areas called continents. Morocco is a country on the continent of Africa.

couscous (KOOS–koos)
Couscous is a dish made with meat, beans, and other vegetables. Many Moroccans like to eat couscous.

mouflon (moo–FLOH)
A mouflon is a wild sheep found in Morocco.

phosphate (FAHS–fayt)
Phosphate is a rock that is mined in Morocco. Phosphate is used to help plants grow and for many other things.

plains (PLAYNZ)
Plains are large, flat or gently rolling land areas with few trees. Morocco has huge plains near its mountains.

souk (SOOK)
A souk is a market where people can buy food and supplies. Many things are sold at Moroccan souks.

Index

Web Sites

Learn more about Morocco:
http://www.lonelyplanet.com.au/dest/afr/mor.htm
http://www.infoplease.com/ipa/A0107800.html
http://www.geographia.com/morocco

Listen to Morocco's national anthem:
http://www.emulateme.com/sounds/morocco.mid

Learn more about souks:
http://www.maghreb.net/countries/morocco/souks.html

Learn more Arabic words:
http://www.travlang.com/languages
(Then be sure to click on the word "Arabic.")